SALLY KNIGHT

Guru Sal

AUSTIN MACAULEY PUBLISHERS™

LONDON • CAMBRIDGE • NEW YORK • SHARJAH

A CIP catalogue record for this title is available from the British Library.

ISBN 9781035836734 (Paperback)
ISBN 9781035836741 (ePub e-book)

www.austinmacauley.co.uk

First Published 2024
Austin Macauley Publishers Ltd®
1 Canada Square
Canary Wharf
London
E14 5AA

For my parents Kate and Michael. David, my husband and my inspiration. For my beloved children Howard and Susie. For my beautiful family Gemma, Paul, Jamie, Liam, Annabelle, Ryan, Liam and Neil. And any future grandchildren.

For all my glorious girlfriends and for my sister in all but blood, Liesel.

To my publishers Austin Macauley for having faith in 'Guru Sal' and to my inspiration, my husband David.

CONTENTS

GURU SAL

Guru Sal is a wise woman in the modern world. One who has been gifted with valuable insight and eternal wisdom. Guru Sal has walked the paths of female angst herself and now seeks to assist her Sisters of the world and guide them to their own solutions to their issues. Not all in this world is rosy, not everything is easy for a woman or girl. BUT, with the help of Guru Sal, Sisters will have the support of a woman who has the knowledge and intuition to help you overcome your personal issues and make your life easier. Whether it is your man, your workload or just wanting more of life's simple pleasures, Guru Sal will strive to help you achieve exactly what you desire through her own expertise and subjectivity – all in your favour, of course!

Guru Sal invites Sisters to write in with problems and in time she will respond with assertive, no-nonsense solutions. Names and places will be changed to protect privacy.

Power to my wily Sisters!

Guru Sal

MY TIPS FOR AN EASY LIFE

Hello Sisters!

I am here to make your life easy. I admit it has taken me a few years, but I have worked out how to make my daily life easier. My tips are tried and tested, and I want to share these with you, precious Sisters of the world. Continue to write to me with your issues and I will endeavour to help you.

My current tip of the month is for you to make it appear to your old man that you are working hard and pulling your weight in these trying times... when we know that probably isn't the case at all.

So, when your man is out at work, busy in the garden or doing the essential shop, you must seize the opportunity to grab your favourite book, or (for the naughty among you) your favourite tipple. Position yourself nice and comfortably near a window overlooking the main road or your garden. Put your feet up and indulge yourself in a few hours of relaxation. Have your Mr Sheen polish and an old rag by your side. Better still, have two rags on the go and ensure they are nice and dirty. Ensure, though, that you have a good view of your man's return to the house and be sure to give yourself enough time to suddenly spring up from your point of relaxation and look busy with those dirty rags. For the Sisters amongst us who own a dog, tell the dog to bark excitedly to warn you of their master's return, just in case you happen to nod off, and have a Bonio at the ready to reward your faithful friend.

Have your vacuum situated close by and plugged in, preferably with the ON button close to your foot. This way, he can be sure you have done or are in the middle of doing something productive around the house. You do not actually have to vacuum. No, Sisters, all you need to do is make some authentic looking 'vacuum marks' on the carpet. You can use a fork or your fingernails for this. This makes it look as if you have been vacuuming all around the house. There seems to be nothing more pleasing to the simple male than the distant sound of the vacuum cleaner. It seals in his small mind that his woman is hard at it, shining his castle until it positively gleams for him to come home to and settle down in come eventide.

So, getting back to your book or tipple – or both! – settle yourself down; a nice warm blanket and fluffy cushions help you to a nice relaxing afternoon.

Have a little nap if you feel the need to. God knows, girls, you deserve that! ENJOY!

It is a good idea, the night before you plan your relaxing day at home, to put out a large clean pile of clothes, towels and sheets in plain sight of your man. Even better if he trips over it all. That way, he will know you are about to embark on a serious day of housework.

Ensure you mention at every opportunity the multitude of tasks ahead of you and wonder (out loud, of course) how on earth you are ever going to get through it all. You might, at this stage, throw in the fact that your back aches and you are feeling a trifle nauseous, but no matter: you, the fine strong woman that you are, will 'soldier on'.

Wherever you wander around your house, it is wise to carry with you an empty but large washing basket. That way, he will know for sure you either intend to do, are doing, or have done (and obviously put away) that huge load of washing. At the close of day, girls, it is an easy thing to pop a pile of whatever back in the cupboards. Drop an odd sock on the floor. That way, he will deduce you have had to carry a truly heavy load during the day and as such will have been occupied in a most pleasing manner.

As we all know, you are Wonder Woman! Your man is going to want to settle down after a day at work to a nice home-made tea, is he not? Well, listen up ladies, blow that for a game of soldiers!

This is what you do.

Pop to the freezer and get out a pizza. Rootle around the bin for a bit of last week's tomato and leave it on the countertop with a bit of yesterday's cheese rind, which will also be in the bin. Smear a bit of flour over your cheeks and nose. Not only will you look sexy and appealing, he will also cast his eyes around the kitchen and think you have made the pizza from scratch! You clever thing, you!

Oh yes, Sister. What a woman you will be in his eyes. He will think you have spent the day doing terrible household chores AND found the reserves to make him a traditional hand-made Italian pizza. (Hail, my wily Sisters!)

Now go ahead and open that expensive bottle of wine you want. There is no way on earth he will moan and deny you that teensy reward. If he does, though, you have my full permission to raise that bottle and bring it down on his ungrateful bonce. But honestly, I do not think you need fear this. Go ahead, Sisters, enjoy that plonk!

However, girls, there could be a slight downside to this. You have 'slaved' all day for that man, and you are bone-weary. Unfortunately, you are going to look cute and sexy with that smear of flour on your cheeks and he now has a belly full of pizza and wine. He is bound to now want 'rumpy-pumpy'.

This is something I know we are all keen to avoid. So, listen up well, my Sisters. You now have three options.

1. If he is a man you can reason with, you tell him how hard you have worked all day. You have washed, cleaned, dusted and ironed like your life depends on it, just look at the state of those nails. AND you have made him a home-made pizza from scratch. You are just too weary to submit your worn-out body to him tonight. You tell him you need a rest – at this point suggest a luxury weekend away, if you like. Only when you are fully rested after your weekend away could you contemplate giving him 'your best'.
2. Add a healthy splash of vodka to his wine and hope he nods off and forgets the whole evening.
3. Paint a little blue and mauve eyeshadow in the sockets of your eyes, rub a bit of 'eau-de-bin-juice' around your neck, add way too much garlic to your side of the pizza and fart as loudly as you can all night – a dead cert to put him off!

Sisters in my life, heed my words and heed them well. Guru Sal's tips work. Well, what do you think I have been doing all day, eh?

My best to you all,

Guru Sal

ANITA PADD

Dear Guru Sal,

I am not happy because my man is just not handy enough around the house. All the jobs he does are botched and unprofessional. He just does not want to spend money on our place looking nice, but **I** do. How can I resolve this?

Anita Padd

I know what you want, Anita Padd – a neater pad! Ha ha, forgive me, I forget myself.

I am imagining you are an unfortunate Sister with wonky family photos on your walls. Slanting shelves? Tin foil behind radiators? Cling film at those draughty windows? Yes, I thought so. Well, your old boy sounds like a right lazy Scrooge, trying to botch and short-cut and not wanting to do the very thing that he should just do from the start. PAY for professional services. It's a false economy trying to do it himself when he clearly does not have the know-how! Believe me, most men don't, they just think they do.

Now, this is my suggestion for you. Organise a little drinks evening for your Sisters. Beforehand, though, tell them you need their help and it's their job during the evening to pick fault with all your man's handiwork. You may have to provide each Sister with a little 'map' of your home and highlight all of his 'shortcomings'. All your Sisters have to do is – in his presence, of course – criticise it, every last thing.

The simple male hates criticism of any kind, so he is not likely to tolerate this for long. The next thing you need your Sisters to do for you, after their prolonged critique of his shabby handiwork, is to charm him. Now, they need to offer him a little glass of 'Man Brew', tickle his chin and pat the space on the settee for him to park his butt on. They should all gather round and say how wonderful their own men have been in just getting straight to it and ordering in professional services to get their jobs done. Properly. They tell him that all the while their men had the workman round, they plied their own man with 'Man Brew' and the promise of a 'happy' evening. The work eventually gets done; the Sisters are happy. The best thing is, though, is that he will be too drunk to remember his promise of a 'happy evening' or he will fall asleep and forget everything. Happiness all round, I say. And that, my dear Sister, is how you get yourself a neater pad!

Guru Sal

CHEF

Dear Guru Sal,

I work full-time and I'm on my feet from dawn until midnight non-stop. I get my man his breakfast before I leave for work. I pack his lunch and I make him his tea as soon as I get home from work. He never helps with the meals and I am so very tired of it all. What advice do you have for me?

Barbara Bakewell-Knott

I know, Barbara: making the evening meals, day in, day out, is quite a drag, isn't it? And you say you get him breakfast too? You need to re-think that one, Barbara my dear Sister. Well, listen to me, Sisters of the world. Here is a little tip you could try out. It has worked for me, so do test it out for yourselves.

Over the next few weeks, together with your man, watch on TV *Ready Steady Cook, Master Chef, Bake Off* or anything else food-related that takes your fancy. Tell him during every episode how much you admire a man who can cook up fantastic meals from scratch and look sexy doing it.

Invite your fellow Sisters around for drinks one evening, telling them you require their help (you will be doing it for each other in no time). Agree between you all that evening meals are a real chore and that Guru Sal has discovered a neat little trick to solve this.

Each Sister will pick a celebrity chef their man looks most like. Someone among you will have a short gingery chap who resembles Anthony Worral Thompson; someone's man could look like Ainsley; some lucky Sister could have a man who looks the spit of James Martin; another's could look a little like Heston? You get the gist. When your man walks in to serve you and your Sisters drinks and nibbles, all the ladies must flatter your man, saying he looks just like (whoever the chef may be) and that they bet he is a real 'sexy whizz' at the oven. Watch as your man melts at all the flattery. (Men are silly, aren't they?) Then you will bolster up their flattery by explaining to your Sisters your man has made the most fabulous meals in the past and that he has a skill that really needs reviving. You will then, at this point and in your man's presence, invite all your Sisters round for a four-course, slap-up meal one night to showcase your man's skills. He may feel under a little pressure, so gee up your Sisters into slinging him more flattery. Now, make the date for several months ahead, as this will give your man time to practise his talents – and of course you will be having all your meals prepared for you every evening from now on.

Once in a while, you must go into the kitchen and tenderly stroke his forearm and whisper how sexy he is when teasing those spectacular sauces into life. Careful now, a tickle of the forearm only, or this could easily get out of hand. Guru Sal suggests you lay the table with a smouldering smile just to show willing. But you must praise, praise, praise, at every step, and I tell you, girls, you will have your evening meals tenderly prepared for the rest of your lives. Bon Appetit Sisters!

Guru Sal

DISHWASHER DEMON

Guru Sal,

I hate emptying the dishwasher and I just do not want to do it anymore. What can you suggest for me?

Debbie Doless from Derby

Debbie, my poor Princess. Of course, a beauty like yourself was not born to such menial tasks. Think of those beautiful nails: criminal to even think they might flake! No. Guru Sal won't hear of it, Debbie. This is what you do – just make sure you have not been drinking before you even contemplate this ploy. Be your most vulnerable self, approach your man with tears in those very large, soft eyes and swear on all that is holy that every time you complete this task you always see a pair of menacing red eyes looking at you from the dark depths of the dishwasher. Tell him this happens every time you try to empty it and you try so hard to be brave, but the time has come where you can't, just can't, carry out this task anymore. Tell him you are afraid, very afraid. It is having a terrible effect on your anxiety. Now is the time to sacrifice a glass, or plate if you must, so drop that glass! Is this happening to other Sisters? I am certain that it is. Mark my words, girls, no decent man would condemn you to that duty ever again. You are safe. Now, after that fright, ladies, you need to recover. Tickle your man under the chin. Careful now, a chin tickle is all that is required at this stage. Whisper grateful thanks in his ear. If you feel you can, a little lick of said ear will help your cause further. It is a sure fact that, after banning you from that fearful task in future, he will leap up from his chair and prepare you a very large G&T and order complete rest and relaxation for the remainder of the day!

Cheers, Debbie!

Guru Sal

BEACHY HEAD

Dear Guru Sal,

My man is driving me mad. I've done nothing but cook, clean and have unwilling sex all through Lockdown and beyond. Am I appreciated? No, I am not! I need a break, please help.

Claire from Clacton

Sister! How much of a break do you want?

He sounds like a true git. Here is my tip for you. How's your spending money situation? I suspect he keeps you poor too, you poor lamb. However, think long-term. Can you stretch to a bike? It does not have to be brand new; no Sister, this bike is destined for a one-way journey only. Look in the local rag or online. You are sure to pick up a cheap bike for a few quid. Just make sure it has a good set of tyres and an uncomfortable saddle. The one you have seen has no brakes? Sister, that won't be a problem. Pop along to your local DIY and get yourself some 'Mr Universe Extra Strong Transparent Glue'. Then skip along to the Sat Nav shop and get one of those cheap 'plug-in-your-own-destination-one-use-only' Tom Toms.

Go home with said cycle and, just before your man returns from his errand, busy yourself in the garage. First, fix the Tom Tom securely to the handlebars – I can't stress how important this is – and set in the destination... **'Beachy Head'**. Now glue up the saddle well. Clear glue offers a nice glossy look. The thicker the application the better, plus it will look like you have done a good job polishing up the saddle for your ungrateful git. He will be pleased. If there is a little bit of spare glue, just wipe it around the handlebars and foot pedals. Now, tell him this is your gift to him and that you'd be delighted if he sat on it and let you see him go off for a little ride.

He will mount the bike in a jiffy to test out his new toy; you will have set the destination – **Beachy Head** – and he will be firmly stuck to the saddle. Now, wave him off with a little air kiss with the promise that while he is gone you are going to prepare him a nice little supper. Oh, he won't be coming back? Then the little supper will serve as a useful wake!

Enjoy your 'break', Sister! You are free!

Guru Sal

TUMBLE DRYER

Dear Guru Sal,

Can you believe this? My man bought me a tumble dryer the other day because I was fed up with hanging all the clothes on the line and the wind blowing them off onto the grass so they got muddy again. Either that or on wet days I must hang them on our radiators! Anyway, along came the lovely new tumble dryer, but now my man tells me not to use it because it is too expensive.

Whatever can I do?

Peggy Lynes

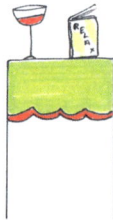

Ah Peggy, have you been partaking in a spot of laundry lately? Me too, and I am most fond of any labour-saving device. Tell your mean bloke that it is a false economy not to get the job done. If you have to re-wash all your laundry when it falls from the line, then what a lot of water and soap powder you waste.

However, here is a tip I would like to share with you. In the olden days, our grandmothers would spend ages wiping down the washing line, fixing pegs and hanging out the said washing, watching out for bird-splattings, battling with sheets in the wind then spending too long at the window keeping an eye out for rain so they would never have any time to rest and continue reading their book of choice.

We don't need to do that, do we? No, regardless of the weather and even if it is sunny outside, there is no need for you to waste time doing any of the above. We use tumble dryers these days, don't we? A tumble dryer is a good labour-saving contraption, and it tends to save on the ugly task of ironing too. If you catch the clothing when it has just dried, you can fold a tee shirt and then just spread your hands over the front part that shows and, hey presto, it looks ironed. However, Sisters, one word of warning. You do not do this in front of your man. We all know he does not like the tumbler to be used much, if at all. He yells, 'It's expensive!' I ask you this, Sisters, 'why did he buy it, then?' So, the best thing to do is wait until your man has gone out for a while, then quickly set to putting the tumbler to work. You will get that washing dried in a jiffy, so while it is working away you settle down to a nice glass of your fancy and your book. My tip here, though, especially for you, Peggy dear, is that at this point you get out the iron and ironing board anyway and open the window a little to let the warm air out. (We do not want the old man detecting a sudden increase in temperature, do we?) On his return, just plug in the iron for a few moments to make it look like it has been used, empty the dryer and quickly fold up the clothes into the basket and head on upstairs just as he enters the house. He will be satisfied that you have been occupied in a most industrious manner. Ruffle up your hair a bit then come downstairs looking flushed and utterly worn out. Mark my words, Sisters, he will suggest a take-out meal for you tonight!

Well done, my wily Sisters.

Guru Sal

TEACHER SUE

Dear Guru Sal,

I'm having trouble with my 'little man' boss at work, he is such a bully. I'm a poetry teacher. What to do?

Sue from Swindon

Dear Sue,

I sympathise! I have had much experience of similar situations in my working life, and I know you'll probably be anxious for my swift reply so here it comes (in a style I know you will appreciate).

You go to work to do a job,
But get obstructed by a knob!
Doesn't it just make you sick,
Little man with little dick?
Tries to come on all hard and strong,
We girls know he's very wrong!
So here it is, my tip for you,
You're the best, you know it, Sue!
So, go ahead as you are,
The kids all treat you like a star,
And that's the most important thing,
Do NOT kowtow and give in to him!
Sister Sue, soldier on,
I know you haven't got it wrong.
He's a twat, that's for sure,
And will be so for evermore.
So, fight the fight with all your might
And conquer men of little height!

Guru Sal

THE iRON

Dear Guru Sal,

My man moans when I have ironed his clothes. Every time he pulls out a nicely ironed shirt from his wardrobe, he complains that I have not taken out all the creases. Oh, Guru Sal, I have too much to do without spending hours on end on one shirt. I don't know how I can solve this problem. Please help.

Rita from Rochester

Rita! What a tedious little man you have there. It's time to rectify this for good. Now listen to me. I know how long it takes us Sisters to partake in that mind-numbing job when really there are so many other pleasures in life. Now, Christmas is not that far off, so have a little sit-down; why don't you have a little glass of whatever you fancy? A glass or two helps you to make good decisions! Now, think about the gifts you would like to get. Make a list.

My suggestion to you is that YOU will definitely need a new iPhone; you've had that old one for years and it's time to step into the modern world. While you are at it, I recommend you treat yourself to that new iPad you've coveted lately. Go on, Sister, you deserve it. Oh, you are starting to feel a little guilty about what to get the old man? Well, let's get back to the reason you are writing to me in the first place. A man who constantly moans about creased shirts and trousers and now says he would like his socks and pants ironed too? I don't think so! Guru Sal knows just the thing and I am going to guide you gently to the solution. Now, peruse at your leisure from that lovely new iPad of yours and you will find him the perfect gift. A new hobby, perhaps? Something to keep him occupied for hours? A sure thing to cease all that moaning? Something he doesn't even know he wants yet?? Yes! You have it! Order him the latest top-of-the-range iRon! Make sure you purchase the newest iRon, you know, the one with plenty of buttons and pretty lights. In fact, my own dear friend bought her man a very top-of-the-range iRon that plays tunes!! The simple male loves a gadget, does he not?

Mark my words, Sister, he will be so delighted and enthralled by the music, lights, sound effects (hissing steam) and the multitude of buttons that he will just rush to get out his creased clothing to test out his new toy! But the bonus for you here is that he will be keen to iron *your* clothes too. Before long, he will become completely addicted to his gleaming new iRon, so you will have more time on your hands to enjoy the pleasures in your life: your book or your chilled Chardonnay, perhaps?

Happy New Year, Happy New You, Sister!

Guru Sal

ROSIE PUDGE

Dear Guru Sal,

My man is complaining I am fat. It's true I have taken to a bit of comfort eating in these last few months, especially during Lockdown, but I'm not that bad. I might just say that I am cuddly, that's all. What shall I do? He keeps going on.

Rosie Pudge

Oh Sister, I suspect your man is no 'slim Jim' himself? Fancy berating you in this way. Now, there may not be too much we can do instantly here, but bear with me and let's see if we can give you a few solutions.

I might suggest to you that if you want to lose a bit of timber then you may have to diet. If you are not keen on that idea – and to be honest, Rosie dear, why should you be? No! Now you could try these few tips. Does your man take sugar in his coffee? Well, increase it by another spoonful. Be kind and tell him you will be making all his hot drinks for the foreseeable future. You can buy yourself bottles of fizzy drink. You can have the diet stuff yourself, or not, but keep the diet bottle back and fill it up with regular fizz and ply him with the stuff. I know for certain, no-one can really taste the difference. I'm sure by now you will have managed to get your man to do his own packed lunches but now is the time to kindly offer to take the stress out of his day and prepare his yourself. Ply his sandwich box with plenty of thick buttered rolls and add large slabs of cheese with sugar-laden chutneys. Fling in a fruit flan with plenty of cream! In time he will become completely addicted and be proud that you attend to his gastronomic needs.

Has he got a gym card? Burn it! Does he cycle to work? Pop his tyres! Drip a little drop of dwale in his cup of tea when he comes home from work; he's sure to fall straight to sleep (ensure you give him his calorie-packed tea first). Plump up his cushions to make his easy chair harder to rise from and it's a good idea, summer or no, to turn up the heating a notch. He will drowse his evenings away, Rosie. Mark my words, my lovely Sister.

Next, loosen his buttons on his clothing and discreetly add a little teeny bit of elastic to his waistbands if you can. OK, it may require a little work on your part, Rosie my dear, but listen, you can take the weight off your feet and have a nice little sit-down with your needle and thread. You may not be able to read your latest novella whilst sewing BUT you can listen to a nice audiobook, can you not? Guru Sal suggests making this task a little more bearable; so, a nice large G&T would help a treat!

In time, Rosie my dear, he will become a fat, lazy git and he will NOT be moaning at you any longer. You have two choices here: you can either let him catch up with you weight-wise and be content (anything to stop his dreary moaning). Or you could run off into the night, lose your pounds, and who knows, you may even run into the man of your dreams?

I give you my best.

Guru Sal

DORA DO-NOWT

Dear Guru Sal,

I work hard all week, but my man expects a long lie-in at the weekends AND for me to make him a full English breakfast with all the trimmings. I just do not want to be doing this job anymore. It's not as if he ever thanks me. I'm fed up with it all, please help me.

Dora Do-Nowt from Derby

Dora! And all Sisters who this dodgy situation applies to. I'm guessing, Sisters, that many of us suffer from this burden. Well, I'm going to suggest to you to be a dutiful wife or partner, offer to make your lazy man a good old-fashioned English fry-up. Offer breakfast in bed if you must. Sisters, you will only ever need to do this task once. This is what Guru Sal suggests.

First, fry up the mushrooms in a whole lot of lard and then leave to chill in the fridge. Meanwhile, plonk those big fat sausages in the oven and cook on high for an hour or two. Whilst you are at it, flop a few rashers of bacon in with the sausages. Now then, the last thing you want to be doing is to be frying eggs, so now is the time to drop in a couple of eggs into a pan of boiling water.

Again, they can come out with the sausages and bacon, so an hour or two should do the trick.

Now Dora, sweetheart, you must be tired, so go on, put your feet up, have a nice cup of tea and a read of your lovely new book. When you feel adequately rested, get up and check the contents of the oven. Do the sausages look like they have been through a crematorium? Do the bacon rashers look slab-like and charred? Then they are done. Get a nice cold plate from the cupboard and neatly arrange the sausages, bacon and hard-boiled eggs and the chilled mushrooms from the fridge. 'What's that white stuff clinging to the mushrooms?' I hear you say. Don't worry, girls, it's called 'pretty mushroom frosting'. Tell your man it's all the rage in Heston's restaurants. Oh, you forgot the baked beans? Don't worry, Heston says cold baked beans are the *haute cuisine* of the breakfast world, so just plop them on straight from the tin. If you prefer, you could disguise the blackest parts of the sausages with a plop of ketchup. (You could end up wasting a lot of ketchup Sisters, so put the ketchup back, he really isn't worth it.) Now, you are ready to serve this lovingly nurtured breakfast up to your man with your best smile and a winning shimmy of those sexy hips. Shimmy on around your man and blow air kisses. Be careful now, no more than air kisses are required at this stage. We can't risk him getting carried away.

Dora, just leave him to it. He won't have the nerve to complain, what with all your shimmying. He won't even attempt to eat his breakfast, so ensure there is a bin close by to spare him the embarrassment of you witnessing him dumping it.

I guarantee you this, Sisters, never again will you be asked to cook up a breakfast feast; it will surely be your last. This is something to celebrate, so go ahead, enjoy an early morning Prosecco in private.

Not only could this be your last breakfast, if you carry my tips over to lunches and dinners, who knows, you could be heading out for more treats at local pubs! And you know what normally accompanies meals out? Yay! Wine!

Cheers to you, Dora, and to our other suffering Sisters.

Power to the Sisters! Stay strong and wily, girls, for with Guru Sal's help you WILL have an easy life!

Guru Sal

DRIVING MISS DAISY

Dear Guru Sal,

My man complains ALL the time about my driving! I either drive too slow or too fast, or else I unnecessarily brake too hard. Oh, Guru Sal, there is nothing wrong with my driving, but I cannot carry on with him demeaning my driving skills like this. Please help me. I am a gibbering wreck.

Daisy Driver

Daisy, my poor lamb. What a turd you have there! Well, I know there is nothing wrong with your driving. With my help, you can keep your driving licence clean AND get yourself ferried about everywhere, how do you fancy that? Appealing? I thought so. This is what you do.

Early one morning, before your turd rises, pop outside and cast birdseed all the way along your street. Now, when it is time to leave for work, drive up your road and you will find the birds will all be getting in your way. This is the time to brake several times as HARD as you can so that his safety belt can hardly keep him from banging his head against the windscreen. In fact, turn this into a little game for yourself. See how many brakes it takes for him to bang his head on the windscreen! He will get mad and call you lots of unprintable names. Go ahead, Daisy, clip the curb and do your best to scuff those silver wheel trims – you know, the ones men are so keen to avoid scratching. Mark my words, my dear, he will snatch away those car keys and shout that you are unfit to be on the roads. Now bear with me here, Daisy; just take a deep breath and hand the keys over; tremble like a jelly then tell him you agree with him. YES! This time you actually agree with him. He will be taken slightly aback at this, he may even shut up, but I'm telling you, Daisy, this is for your own good. He will now insist he be the one to drive you both off to work and back from now on. Now, when it comes to the weekly shop, he will no doubt say you are too dangerous to be driving so he will do the shopping from now on. That's good for you, as you can now settle down with your latest book and have a sneaky glass or two.

Now, there could be a small downside to this. How are you going to get out and about and have fun with all your Sisters? Daisy, I ask you this. Can you put your book aside for at least an hour a day and wine? Pardon me, I forget myself. I meant, can you put your book aside for at least an hour and go for a full-on whine? You can? Excellent. The simple male cannot stand to be whined at for too long. Keep this up and he will be only too pleased to take you to wherever it is you want to go so he can have a day's peace. Daisy! Think of all that shopping you can do, the lunch dates you need to keep. Think of all those wine bars! Daisy, this is your personal taxi service for the rest of your life. Guru Sal's advice here, though, is to keep a spare set of keys hidden, for emergency outings!

Guru Sal

DUSTING DILEMMA

Guru Sal,

I don't want to do the fruitless task of dusting. Ever again!

Hazel Dolittle from Dorchester

GRIMY GLASSES

GURU SAL OFFICIAL STUDY

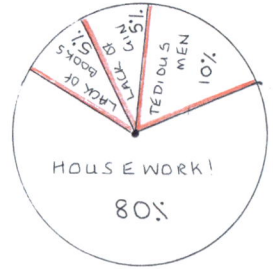

LACK OF BOOKS
LACK OF GIN 5%
TEDIOUS MEN 10%
HOUSEWORK!
80%

ITEMS OF DETRIMENT TO UK WOMEN
AT THIS MOMENT IN TIME ... OFFICIAL!

TAKE A BREAK

VINO

MY SHEEN

OLD RAGS

Hazel, I have recently conducted a survey into the lives of the modern Sister. Though I have suspected this for many years what do you think I discovered? The biggest killer of Sisters in the United Kingdom is actually unpaid HOUSEWORK. It is an activity I am keen to avoid myself and strongly advise other women to do the same.

Here's my solution for you. Lightly spray the old man's specs with a greasy film and shake an old duster over them. That way he won't even notice the house needs a good spruce-up. Tell the old man his work rival's wife has cleaners. You know your old man likes to keep up with his co-workers, so suggest to him he needs to poach these cleaning operatives. Meanwhile, you may have to develop a new style of language. A good phrase could be, 'Darling, while you're gone, I'll give the house a thorough dusting...' This translates as: 'While you're out, I'll cast an eye over the house for dust and if I see any I'll just blow it about a bit.' Why, he won't even notice a thing with his new specs. Run around the house with some lavender room spray and he'll think you've been at it all day. You never know, he may feel a pang of guilt at his colleague having cleaners and not you — you poor over-worked lamb. He's bound to take a little pity on you and fix you up with a white wine spritzer. Actually, ask him to forget the 'spritzer' part (unfortunately you know how over-generous he can be with that). Tell him you'll settle for an extra-large glass of the best Chardonnay. Just wait, he'll be poaching those cleaners in a jiffy!

My best,

Guru Sal

DAYDREAMING

Dear Guru Sal,

My man complains because he says I daydream and do not listen to a word he says. What can I do? I'm fond of a little daydream and my man does have a tendency to prattle on. Please help me.

Emma T. Head

Sister! What a dreary bloke you have there! Does he not realise the most creative people in the world daydream? A lot. Of course, you don't actually 'forget' what he says – no, you have just 'switched off'. I completely understand; I'm guessing he rather goes on a lot? Am I right?

Well, no wonder you do not catch every little thing he says. What he says, and this is true of most of the male kind, mainly consists of nothing but moaning, so of course it is natural for you to just 'zone out'.

Now then, a solution is needed for you, Emma. I suggest you tell your man you have been to the doctor who has diagnosed you with a severe case of Omphaloskepsis. The doctor says that the only way to attempt to mend those erratic neurons in the brain is for daily rest. Now my dear, between you and me this is nothing whatsoever to concern yourself over. Omphaloskepsis is a scientific term for 'navel-gazing'. However, the simple male will not know this, nor will he bother to find out. Suffice it to say, if it is too difficult for him to pronounce then it must be a serious complaint. You tell him that you may, and only may, recover from this ailment, BUT that you need time out of your busy day for rest. Bedrest if at all possible – nowhere more comfortable, in my opinion. Then tell him the doctor says that a couple of drops of laudanum in your tea will be a useful aid to true relaxation and brain repair. Emma, you can daydream away in Technicolor for as long as you wish, my dear.

Alternatively, though possibly not quite as potentially rewarding, tell your man that after a visit to the doctor and a referral to the audiologist, you are going deaf. Of course, you are not losing your hearing but, again, the simple male will not know that. It may even fill him with remorse for the fact he has berated you lately – and we all know what a little bit of guilt does to a man, don't we, Sisters? Yes, gifts! So be prepared for a temporary showering of gifts. Big or small, receive them gratefully with a big smile and a little air-kiss. Be careful here, we don't want him to get carried away or even begin to feel he has been forgiven. Enjoy these gifts while they last.

Then show him those little twin 'hearing aids' the audiologist has prescribed for you. Only the best will do, and they can come to a whopping £2k or £3k! Ask your man to fund the hearing aids and a bank transfer will do nicely, thank you, then get him to give you the cash to insure them. Now, you know and I know, these are not hearing aids per se. No, they are some bog-standard, colour-neutral earplugs. Pop them in from time to time, preferably when his prattling starts, and he will be able to see that you are actually using them. These little beauties will serve as a great defender to his incessant moaning.

And Sister, do not forget your new healthy bank balance. You now have money to spend and enjoy. Remember, if funds start to dwindle, you can ask your man for the next annual insurance payment. Oh, the insurance has rocketed over the past year? Fantastic news! Or, tell him your new little friends will need 'upgrading' regularly if you are to truly benefit – you know what I am saying, Sister?

Emma, I give you my best. I said, 'I GIVE YOU MY BEST!'

Guru Sal

FALINE DA FLUSCHE

Dear Guru Sal,

I am 56 and am halfway through my menopause. Lately, though, I have been very troubled by night sweats and hot flushes. My man says it's all 'in my mind' and to 'crack on' because he thinks I am faking it. I assure you this is not the case, Guru Sal.

Please help me.

Faline Da Flusche

Faline! I am with you on this one and can wholeheartedly confirm this is not in your mind: It is real and very inconvenient. What a cheek – I'll give him 'crack on'! Your ignorant man needs re-educating on this score.

Here is my shopping list for you: one long thin pole with a small, hooped end, two pieces of rope, a large, feathered fan (punkah wallah style), the latest bestseller and a bottle of your favourite gin. In your bedroom, vertically fasten the hooped pole securely to the ceiling. Thread the two pieces of rope through the hoop, attach the large, feathered fan to one end of the rope and the neck of the bottle of gin to the other. Then set your book, gin and a large glass, with ice, on your bedside table.

Call your man up to the room and attach the other two ends of the rope to each of his big toes. Now, dear lady, lie down and relax. Tell him to 'crack on' and 'mark time' for at least an hour. Tell him if he wants to get you 'up and running' again, as it were, he must 'crack on' and co-operate. Besides, you can tell him he will benefit too, as this exercise with give him the sexy quads he's always coveted. You, my dear hot girl, will benefit twice over as you will be constantly cooled by the said fan and have yourself a drink regularly poured out to keep you hydrated.

During this relaxing hour, you should use the time to peruse those very expensive holiday brochures. You tell him where in the world you want to go and don't forget to tell him how much this will all cost! After a few 'hot sweats' of his own he will come to understand how rotten he has been towards you and start treating you properly, my dear Faline. Now, my sweet Sister, this can go on for as long as you so desire or at least until his attitude changes; the power is now entirely in your hands.

My best to you, Sister.

Guru Sal

MENIZA HERTZ

Dear Guru Sal,

I am 52 and am going through the Menopause. I can't do the housework as well as I used to as all my joints are so stiff! My man says I'm just being lazy, but believe me, this is not the case. What can I do? Please help.

Meniza Hertz

Meniza! What is your man thinking? I am shocked at his thoughtlessness and ignorance. Well, here is my remedy for you. You must take a trip to your local 'alternative health' shop and stock up on cod liver oil, evening primrose oil and a large bottle of Aqua Vitae. Do you have a joint, pardon the pun, bank account? If so, then this is your next step. You must immediately order one of those top-of the-range-vibrating-massaging-warming-beds. I prescribe for you to relax and take things easy every day for as long as you need. You need a regular dose of your oils quaffed down with large swigs of Aqua Vitae; now do not worry about the regular consumption of the Aqua Vitae as it hails from the health shop, so no worries there. Whilst you are relaxing on your top-of-the-range-vibrating-massagingwarming-bed, you can look through the list of local cleaners and hire one with immediate effect!

Blessings,

Guru Sal

MATITZA AKITU

Dear Guru Sal,

I am 54 and I am going through the menopause. My breasts ache so much I can hardly walk, let alone do a day's work. Please help me.

Matitza Akitu

Ahh, Matitza. Let me guess, a Sister from Japan, perhaps? Then welcome to our forum. Well now, I understand this problem so well. What you need to do straight away is order yourself a lovely day bed. You must, under no circumstances, even think of doing a hard day's work.

Now, just you relax on your day bed and let the world go by. Perhaps you have a collection of the latest reads from Banana Yoshimoto? You must accompany these great reads with a bottle of *sake*. Yes, that should do the trick. Wrap your aching mammaries in cooled leaves of the common cabbage and allow those healing properties to work their magic and soothe those throbbing mounds. This problem will pass in its own good time. However, in the meantime, get your man to hire you a house cleaner and tell him to leave you be while you convalesce. Warn him, though, that complete recovery could take years. Banana Yoshimoto has written a series of good reads and you will want to catch up on these without interruption!

I give you my best, Sister.

Guru Sal

PIA GALORA

Dear Guru Sal,

I'm of the age now where, when I cough or sneeze, I may do a tiny wee.
Whatever shall I do? Ciao Bella.

Pia Galora from Italy

Pia, my dear, this is normal and completely natural, and you should not worry. There is always a solution to every issue and I, Guru Sal, have the solution for you. Now, you may know I am a fan of nature and greatly admire all animals of our world. I observe animals' habits and ways so I can safely advise you that doing a little wee here and there has huge benefits.

Did you know that in nature, to attract a male partner, the female sloth goes in search of a potential beau? Once she spies a male she fancies, she goes about her daily routine in his vicinity. She knows she has caught him well and truly! She goes about her daily routine but then wanders off and scents her trail with a little cough and, you know, a little wee follows. She knows for sure he will have caught that exotic aroma and, believe me ladies, it is highly exciting for the male to be 'on the scent'. Now, here I must assure you that human males are exactly the same; it's just that they are just too dim to realise. The male sloth is there, I'd like to say in an instant, but he is a sloth, so he will be there in about three weeks. Time for the female to make comfy her nest because when he arrives there will be a show and a half, I can tell you! She is a sex magnet! He is now forever hooked.

So, Pia, my dear, I offer you the secret benefit to your conundrum. One word of warning, though: don't go through the hay fever season on a full bladder. You could get more than you bargained for!

Guru Sal

FANNY GNASHERS

Dear Guru Sal,

I'm fed up! Lockdown has exhausted me and unfortunately my man has not been able to get out and work! Still! He is asking too much sex from me and he's getting on my nerves. Help me or I will go mad!

Muffy Chuffington-Clampdown

Sister, I hear you. I know many Sisters are suffering in this way and I know how annoying this pestering can be. But worry not, I have a remedy for you. Do you still get Sunday newspapers? Oh, you don't? Well, I might suggest you start getting a Sunday tabloid delivery. Look in the back pages. You will find a variety of very strange items for sale there. Items you cannot readily get in the shops these days. Last Sunday, for example, I ordered my man some 'nasal hair strimmers' – he had terrible nasal hair growth which almost met his top lip. Not a great look. The strimmers worked a treat! Nasal hair all gone! He has a constant dripping nose now, though – some things come with a downside.

Anyway, amongst all these odd advertisements I happened upon an intriguing headline, 'Banish Unwanted Advances' and in the smaller print I saw for sale, 'Fanny Gnashers'. The text explained this is a simple device much like a full set of false teeth with a discreet little wind-up key at one end to set the teeth a-gnashing – the more expensive ones come with a timer delay, and I suggest this is what you go for.

The operation is simple. First, throughout the evening ply your man with several bottles of 'Man Brew' – you will discover in due course that this is a handy 'blameworthy' product. Go to bed and slip the device into 'you know where' and wait. Sooner or later your man will plod up the stairs and into the bathroom to 'prepare'. This is the time to wind up your device in readiness. He will slide into bed beside you and start his pawing. Allow him to reach the state of no return. At the point of attempted entry (I'm sure you know what I mean) this is the time to extract that key! Set your fanny a-gnashing!!! At the first nip, he will leap out of bed as quick as a rocket set for the moon! He will run straight back to the bathroom to rub a little cream on his end – or rub cream on his little end? Oh well, you get the gist, Sister. When he returns, his ardour will be well and truly dampened I can assure you. If he even dares to ask what has happened, you just blame it on him having consumed far too much 'Man Brew' and tell him he must be imagining things. Now, my dear girl, Guru Sal's remedy will guarantee you many future restful nights for sure. Remember, repeat every night as necessary and eventually he will give up or at least until his end recovers. Oh, his end has been permanently numbed? That's fantastic news, Muffy!

All the best for future dreamy nights.

Guru Sal

FREE FRIDAY FACIALS FOREVER

Dear Guru Sal,

I was busy creosoting the garden fence because my man was too lazy to do it himself. However, during this activity I splashed my face with a few drops of the creosote. My man is now convinced that I have some permanent facial affliction and as I am now spotty, he thinks I am not as pretty as I once was. What can I do?

Lotta Schwartzkopf

Lotta my dear, what a cheek he has. After all your hard work, too. Well, I'm guessing he is no oil painting himself. But now you have found the benefit of a drop of creosote, you must work this to your advantage. How do you fancy free facials for the rest of your life? Sounds good, doesn't it? Tell your man that he may be right – they love to hear this phrase – and that these 'spots' are due to your age, that you are very distressed about it and you'll do anything to make yourself pretty for him again. Let a little heartfelt tear fall at this point – he will now feel stabs of guilt at upsetting you like this. Tell him that you have discovered a treatment which, in time – but who knows how long this could take? – will cure facial spots. You know perfectly well you do not have acne or anything of the sort, but he is a simple male and will never realise this. He will be glad you will be cured of your spots and will be happy for you to go ahead and book yourself in for the treatment. Guru Sal suggests you find a local salon you like and book in this weekly luxury! Just keep giving yourself an occasional temporary dot over with the 'black stuff' and you will reap the benefits for sure!

My best,

Guru Sal

GARDEN PROBLEM

Dear Guru Sal,

I don't want to do the gardening anymore, please help.

Dorothy Digless

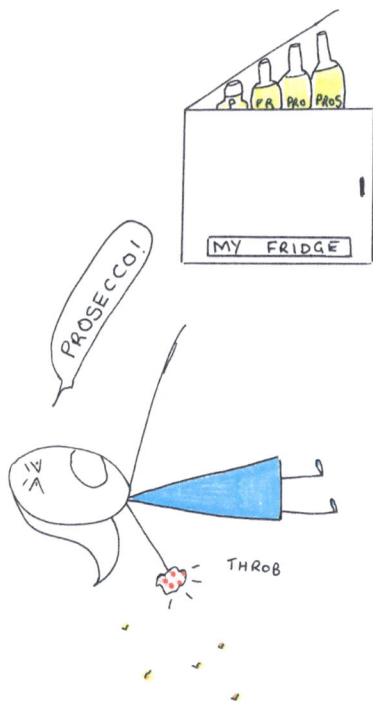

Dorothy! I feel your pain, Sister! Well, let's formulate a plan.

Pop outside to the garden and prepare yourself a basket, secateurs and gloves – you at least have to look like you're setting out for a hard day's work.

Look interested in a pretty plant and decide the garden would benefit with more of these little delights. Offer to research these lovely little flowers and look on your device to assist you. Oh dear, you don't get a signal in your garden. Now you must return to the house and find your book and a pre-prepared Prosecco! Your man will be wholly engrossed in his potting shed for the rest of the day so, go ahead, have a second glass!

Have ready a bright red lipstick hidden in your pocket. Try to smile as you trudge out for another full day of intended work in the garden. After a short while of faffing about at the far end of the garden, give a sudden scream of fright. Quickly apply dots of red lipstick to your hand and shout out that you have inadvertently plunged your hand into what you think is a gang of wasps and that you are allergic to them! Clutch your throat and gasp. Grab your man and whisper those three little words like it will be the final utterance of your life. In a flash, your man will have heaved you over his shoulder in a most manly fashion. He'll tenderly drape you on the sofa and literally beg you to tell him what to get you in order to make you feel better. Did you do a little drama at school? Good, it's sure to come in handy now. In between clutching your throat and those breathy gasps try to get out the first syllable... 'Pro... Pro... Pro...' Then go for the 'full monty'... 'Prosecco!!!' Wave your stung hand shakily towards the fridge. You can be sure, ladies, that your man will be so proud of himself for saving you from anaphylactic shock he's bound to land you the whole bottle! This combined with a full week's rest and the promise of a fortnight's holiday at a destination of your choice come summertime!

Well done, my wily Sister!!

Guru Sal

IMAGINARY FRIEND

Dear Guru Sal,

I have a new man friend; he's nice enough but he seems quite strict and doesn't let me get away with the things my daddy did when I was a little girl. I am an only child and my daddy doted on me. For example, my new chap won't let me have my nightly bottle of Champers or let me have my 'me time.' How can you help me to get over this?

Petulentia Singleton

Pet, my Sister. I can see that you were probably a little Daddy's girl and you are used to having your own way quite a lot. So now, let's see what we can do for you, my dear Pet.

Cast your mind back to when you were a little girl. As an only child, you may not have had a great many friends. So, did you have an imaginary friend? I'm thinking you did, but even if you didn't, now is the time for that friend to appear in your life!

You tell your man that your childhood was traumatic in that you were bereft of playmates, so much so that you had an imaginary friend who did all the things a playmate would. You were inseparable. By the way, Pet, this is a completely normal phenomenon, lots of children do this. Possibly not so common in adulthood, but the average male is not likely to know this.

Your man is bound to feel a flicker of sympathy for you. Start to chatter away to your 'friend' in the kitchen, or anywhere around the house, to be honest. Make sure your man overhears your little conversations. So, when evening comes along, you just go and get yourself a nice cold glass of Champagne, if that is what you want. If your man ventures to question you about this, you must tell him that your friend has recommended this for you. Have a conversation with your friend in front of him. It could go something like this...

You: 'Thank you, I don't mind if I do.'

Then tell your man that your friend (it's nice at this point to name her, as a name creates a bond) has suggested you open a bottle of Champers and that you need to sit back and relax in front of the TV to watch a film of your choice.

This can be used in any situation you choose. So, if you do not feel like cleaning the kitchen, for example, you tell your man that your friend suggests this can be done another day. Take advantage of this, my Sister; put your feet up and rest.

Now, you must be a little careful here, Pet. This sort of behaviour could start to get on his nerves; even the simplest of males may detect when he is starting to be taken advantage of.

The thing to do here is to gradually introduce him to your friend and even though he won't be able to hear what she says (you are the translator here – you are in control of this) you can suggest your friend has taken a shine to him (watch him melt) and that your friend can suggest nice things for him to have too. So, when you want to sit with your bottle of Moët and watch a film, tell him your friend would really like him to partake in a brew of his choice and join you with a film. In no time at all, Sister, you can have all that you want; just let him join in from time to time.

You can have a friend for life there, and although Daddy may no longer be around for you, why should you not feel as spoiled as you once were?

I give you my best, my dear Pet.

Guru Sal

LAZY LINDA

Dear Guru Sal,

I don't want to take the bins out every week. They are very heavy and they smell terrible. Surely this is a man's job?

Lazy Linda from Litchfield

Linda, let's not be too hasty with the prefix of 'lazy'. You have not had very many 'Guru Sal' sessions yet.

But Linda, my Sister, what on earth are you talking about with this bin business? Putting out those stinking great bins is most exclusively a MAN'S job! Tell him most sternly to 'man up' and get out there and do it himself. Utterly refuse, pardon the pun Linda, to partake in this chore again!

Guru Sal

LITTLE MAN DILEMMA

Dear Guru Sal,

I think I have made a mistake. I married my childhood sweetheart. We started going out when we were eight. My problem now is embarrassment. He has hardly grown at all, and although he is a nice chap on the whole, I tower above him and I feel like I am going out with a midget, not a full-grown he-man. Whatever shall I do?

Long Tall Sally

BEFORE...

AFTER...

Sister! Oh, what a predicament. It would be easy to get rid if he were a meany teeny-weeny, but you say he is quite nice – but small. Hmmm, disappointing. Well, I have a plan for you. Try this for size, ha ha. Oh, sorry Sally, I forget myself.

Convince your man to grow his hair. Then take him to your favourite hairdresser for an 'up do'. What you ask for is an up do 'Mr Whippy' style. Then go to town and browse the vintage stalls for a pair of 1973 platforms. Buy them. Next, you purchase him some 'big boy' trousers to hide the platforms, because we all know how stupid they look. With all these in place, you have created the illusion of height with your little man.

Did you know in the Middle Ages a woman was able to rack her man in order to get him to her desired height? These days, though, that notion is considered a trifle harsh. It's a pity racking is no more because it did achieve results. Worry not, Sister, Guru Sal's modern version of the rack is at hand. All you do is take your man for a walk in the local park. Stop in the children's play area where you will find a piece of apparatus that children swing from, 'monkey-style'. Handcuff his wrists to this bar. Then just let him dangle. Once secured in the dangle position you then produce half a dozen bricks; strap three to each ankle. These help to give your man a real good stretching. He won't attempt to cry out – it's a public place, for goodness' sake. He won't want a little kid to notice he can't tolerate a little stretching exercise! And should other children come to play on said equipment, your man will look like any other eight-year-old, so tell him not to feel embarrassed. Tell him he needs to dangle for at least an hour, but not to worry as you will be close by with the handcuff keys.

Now, Sister, go ahead and buy yourself a nice ice cream and settle yourself down on a nearby bench with your new book. If it's a really good read, then you can allow him to dangle for at least eight chapters! Tell him kindly that, as a little man himself, Tom Cruise swears by these one-hour-a-day stretches. If your chap wants to be taller – and mark my words, girls, every little man wants a few extra inches – he will readily agree to this simple regime.

Blessings upon you, Sally.

Guru Sal

MABUTSA BADDUN

Dear Guru Sal,

My man is cross with me because he says I fart too much. He says I offend his senses, especially his nose. What can I do? I can't help myself.

Ms Mabutsa Baddun

Mabutsa! I hear you, Sister. Literally. But listen, your man is ignorant of the benefits of the farting woman. Here's the thing; think of the wind and what comes to mind? Pungent gale forces or soft, breezy, aromatic zephyrs? God created wind. Wind cleanses the atmosphere; its purpose is to blow away stale air and debris. It is natural and completely normal. Now, think on this. Does it not make sense, then, for farts to rush through the rectum in much the same way, blowing away foul microcosms and other anal litter? A fart is nature's Hoover – except in reverse.

Did you know that in nature animals use the act of farting, trumping, guffing – call it what you will – to their great advantage? Let's take the she-wolf, for example. She increases her rank in the wolf pecking order just by farting. The louder, stronger and the more of a stink her flatulence, the more she is admired by her wolf sisters and the more she is desired by the big hungry male wolves – think of a fart as a powerful sexual aphrodisiac. So, tell your man, 'what's not to love?'

Go ahead, Sister, fart away to your heart's content. He'll soon get used to it, mark my words. Perhaps, as an aid, you can use cognitive behavioural therapy (CBT). Start the day off by farting regularly as usual but at a slight distance from your man. Every hour or so, or whenever the 'rumble' takes you, get one step closer to your man and fart away. State the following (kindly if you can, the weak male can find this a trifle traumatic). 'Inhale... hold... and exhale.' After a week or two he'll come to enjoy the exercise and before you know it, he'll take great pleasure in telling you what you had for dinner yesterday.

Now you know the power of a fart, let your botty rip and reverberate to your heart's content, Sister. You need fret no more!

Guru Sal

OENOPHILIA GLOOM

Dear Guru Sal,

When we sit watching the TV at night with a glass of wine, my man always, without exception, only pours me a dribble and takes the rest for himself!

Whatever can I do to make him share, especially the wine!

Oenophilia Gloom

Oenophilia, lovely name – I would love to know the etymology of it. It is shocking to know that a chap could do this to his beloved. This is what you do. Buy yourself a retractable straw! I have many scattered about the house and they work a treat. Firstly, you need to invent a long-term case of 'plantar fasciitis' and every evening, when your foot pain is so great, you have to just keep relaxing on your easy chair and your feet must be raised. Now, set your Alexa up to make doorbell chimes every now and again, and when your old git gets up to answer the door take a nice heavy slurp from his glass with your new friend, the retractable straw! He cannot blame the reduction of his Chateau Lafite on you, no, not with your poorly foot. He will be thinking twice about his alcohol consumption too, because there never seems to be anyone at the front door either. He will quite possibly be thinking about an early appointment with AA. In the meantime, dearest Oenophilia, you may take charge of the wine bottle and the pouring thereof. Don't forget, only the merest dribble for Mr Gloom!

Cheers, Oenophilia!

Guru Sal

SNORING

Dear Guru Sal,

My man SNORES! OMG, every night sounds like a construction site in full swing. I am so very tired; I believe I am on the brink; lack of sleep is literally driving me mad! Oh, Guru Sal, what can I do?

From Sleepless Susie in Sidcup

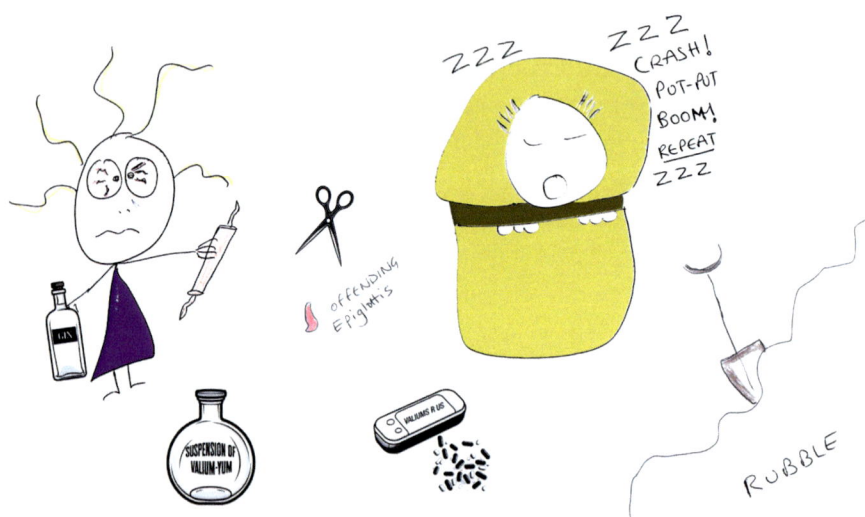

Calm yourself, my Sister. I can cure this problem in a week. I am about to give you seven easy steps to prevent your man's snores – this is a 'graded response approach', so one step at a time, my poor tired lamb.

1. Get yourself some quality earplugs... Oh, you can still hear the dreadful snoring? Go to step 2.
2. Have a few wines before your bedtime; have a few more than usual, get to bed well before your man. The wine should help you drop off nicely... Oh dear, he woke you with an exceptionally loud drilling sound? Go to step 3.
3. As before, have several wines before bedtime (Guru Sal gives you full permission to get absolutely bladdered if you must), but this time take a couple of Valium pills... Oh no, he woke you with those shocking 'Boom-Boom, CRASH' sounds? Go to step 4.

4. Tonight, dear Sister, add a dozen or so crushed Valium pills into his mashed potato; this should knock him out for the count. Just in case, take a rolling pin to bed with you; have it handy, as each time he snores you can 'bop' his bonce with it!!... Oh no, twice as bad? If that could ever be. And he has the gall to complain of an impending migraine? Proceed to step 5.

5. Things are becoming drastic, Sister. Now is the time to be proactive rather than reactive in your response. Clear your head of the previous nights' efforts to control that seismic snore. Take to bed a pair of long scissors and a torch. Have you been watching *Holby* or *Casualty* lately? Good. Now, you are about to perform an epiglottis-ectomy. This could become messy, so have a teacloth handy. Wait until about 3am when the seismic activity is at its worst. Open his trap wide. Use your torch to peer inside his scrag; can you see a little pink flapping thing hanging from the back of his throat? That's your mark – get those long scissors and simply cut off the offending flap! Mop up any 'spills' and try to get some rest if you can... Oh dear, it hasn't worked? He just woke up and said he feels a cold coming on because he has a sore throat AND a headache!? Sling him a Strepsil and send him off to work... You've got some hard thinking ahead of you. What shall you do with the flapping epiglottis? Use it as a dog treat or toss it in his spag bol later. Proceed swiftly to step 6.

6. Now at this point, Guru Sal suggests you have a day off work and collect your thoughts if you can, you poor sweetheart. Have a good look around your house for inspiration. Oh, you can't find anything? Have a look in your garden: a place of solitude, filled with birdsong, plants and pretty things. But oh dear, you did not realise how shabby that patio Is looking. Time to get a new one? Yes, I thought so! Order some slabs, extra heavy will do nicely. Now, Sister, get digging! It will be dark by the time your man gets home so he won't notice that deep hole by the back door. When he comes home, treat him to a final supper – you don't need to spend too much, it won't even make it to the 'recycling', if you know what I mean? Have yourselves a bottle or two of wine, ensure he has the lion's share, though – treat it as your last act of kindness. Go to bed and wait. Sister Susie, this will be your final night of sleeplessness. Listen to those last echoes on the 'construction site' and when it gets to the point of no return use that rolling pin like never before! Go ahead, Sister, let rip! Use all your strength now and heave that big body into the hole and quickly slab over. Job jobbed!

7. You can now both 'Rest in Peace'.

Guru Sal

SCROOGE

Dear Guru Sal,

My man is so stingy he makes Scrooge look like a prodigal spendthrift. How can I tempt him to spend a bit more money on my Christmas presents this year? I feel I deserve a little luxury; I've been hard at it all year.

Last year he bought me a pair of oversized, second-hand socks. When I opened this 'gift', a moth escaped its newspaper captivity with haste!

Please give me some tips, Guru Sal.

Nickey from Nottingham

Oh Nickey, my dear girl! What a miserable miser you have there! My first suggestion would be the number of a decent divorce lawyer! But I'm guessing you feel a teeny bit of affection for your tight-fisted old git? Still, he needs to be taught a lesson. You know lessons from the Guru are the best.

Here is my suggestion for you. Not that he deserves it, but each evening ply your bloke with 'Man Brew'. Whilst he is pushing out the 'ZZZZZ's each evening, search your recycling bin and pull out anything you feel you could wrap up: an empty cereal box, a (clean) baked bean tin, a matchbox. Anything will do, really, because all you are going to do is to gradually set a little wrapped piece of 'rubbish' under your delightful tree, but you must ensure there is a label attached with his name on. Each day when he wakes, he will see his presents literally grow in number under the tree. He should be feeling a touch of guilt by now and he will be thinking about a bit more for you than a pair of charity socks!! I would say that a week before Christmas, start looking for gifts with your name on; you'll be surprised, I'm expecting at least half a dozen to come your way. Then, on Christmas Eve, ply him with mince pies and lots of 'Man Brew', then when you hear that familiar, rhythmical drone, go and chuck all his 'gifts' back in the recycling bin

Come Christmas morning he will have a sore head, see he has no gifts when he could swear blind there were many waiting for him, then he will book in a hasty appointment at AA. You, meanwhile, will enjoy what he has bought for you this year. And, Nickey my dear sweet Sister, if you are not satisfied, just let me know, and that divorce lawyer's phone number will be on your door mat by next post!

Happy New Year.

Guru Sal

WINDOW CLEANING

Dear Guru Sal,

I just hate cleaning the windows. Please advise on how I can get out of it for the rest of my life.

Liesel from Littlehampton.

Liesel! You don't mention your age but I'm assuming you are a lady of maturing years? Am I right? What on earth is your man thinking of, letting you carry on like this, dangerously slaving away –all for the sake of crystal windows?

Darling girl, this is what you do. Wait until your man goes out. Before he leaves, tell him you will start cleaning straight away, working from the highest window first. Wave him off with a smile and then sit down and rest with a nice cup of tea – you've got a bit of planning to do.

Once fully rested, pop to the shed and get out that shaky old ladder, a bucket of water, cloth and rubber gloves. The gloves will make him think you are attacking this task with vigour. Have you got a bit of eye make-up in your bag? Blue and purple are the best colours for this situation. Now, go ahead and be your creative self and powder up your knee in lovely shades of 'big bruise'. Scatter the gloves around nearby and lay the ladder on the floor below the top window. Pop back inside, help yourself to a tipple of your choice and settle yourself down to a nice read. Just be sure to be in full sight of your man's return. A tragedy novella would be a good choice of read here, as when your man returns you will already be crying over the way that wicked villain has treated that poor damsel.

On his return, quickly fold down the page of the book (you'll be sure to be returning to your read very soon) and hide it under the cushion. A good idea at this point would be to have two ice cubes ready: grab them tightly, so when you reach out for your man, he will instantly notice how cold and chilled you have become. Pop outside quickly and kick over the bucket of water and lay yourself awkwardly on the ground next to the ladder. Whimper your man's name like it's the last word you'll ever utter and point weakly to your knee. He will be too concerned about the length of time you've been laying on the cold ground and have anxiety about hypothermia (your hands are like ice, you poor love) to take too much notice of the colour of your knee. He only needs a quick glimpse. He will help you up, gently wrap a bandage around that poor damaged knee and settle you down with your favourite cushion. He will curse himself for trying to save money on you not having a window cleaner and instantly set about rectifying this by appointing one now. He'll breathe a sigh of relief and look lovingly upon his brave, hard-working 'darling' and reflect on his negligence. If you flutter those beautiful eyelashes and let just one tear drop fall, you might get lucky, and he'll rush to get you a nice big glass of red wine; just to help you over the shock and keep the chill out. Go ahead and enjoy this, my Sister; raise your glass in silent toast to your future window cleaner!

Guru Sal